RACE CAR DREAMS

by Sharon Chriscoe

illustrated by
Dave Mottram

RP|KIDS
PHILADELPHIA

ISBN 978-0-7624-5964-3
Library of Congress Control Number: 2015960180

9 8 7 6 5 4 3
Digit on the right indicates the number of this printing

Designed by T.L. Bonaddio
Edited by Marlo Scrimizzi
Typography: Brandon

Published by Running Press Kids
An Imprint of Running Press Book Publishers
A Member of the Perseus Books Group
2300 Chestnut Street
Philadelphia, PA 19103–4371

Visit us on the web!
www.runningpress.com/rpkids

To my family, friends, and agent who dream with me.—S. C.

To my little spark plug, Sara. —D. M.

The zooming has stopped.
The sun's almost set.

A race car is tired.
He's wringing with sweat.

His day has been filled
with high octane fun.
He hugged all the curves.
He's had a good run.

He looks all around.

His friends are now gone.

His engine revs down.

His headlights blink on.

He stretches and yawns
and lets out a sigh.
He rolls off the track
and whispers good-bye.

It's time for his bath.

He heads to the pit.

His wipers are on.

He sweeps off the grit.

TICKLE
AND
WASH

The bubbles tickle as suds start to foam.

He washes his
rims and shines up
his chrome.

All sparkly and clean,
his tummy feels strange.

He lifts up his hood.
It's time for a change.

He guzzles and gulps each dark, oily drop.

His hood slams *ker plunk!* Lights dim in the shop.

He's sleepy and full
and ready to read.

He chooses a book
that's all about speed.

He snuggles his wrench
as the moon shines bright.
The little stars twinkle
and dance in the night.

A gentle wind blows. The air starts to chill.
He turns on the heat and warms up his grill.

Then toasty and warm,
he burrows down deep.

He closes his book and drifts off to sleep.

His engine now hums.
He lets out a snore.
His bumpers relax
and sprawl on the floor.

He throttles the gas.
He shifts into gear.
He smiles and punches
out from the rear.

He zips and he zooms, sweet dreams of the race.
He vrooms to the front . . .

and takes home first place!